Railway Rabbits

Bramble and the Easter Egg

The
Railway
Rabbits

Bramble and the Easter Egg

Georgie Adams

Illustrated by Anna Currey

Orion
Children's Books

First published in Great Britain in 2011
by Orion Children's Books
a division of the Orion Publishing Group Ltd
Orion House
5 Upper St Martin's Lane
London WC2H 9EA
An Hachette Livre UK Company

1 3 5 7 9 10 8 6 4 2

Printed in Great Britain by
Clays Ltd, St Ives plc

ISBN 978 1 4440 0159 4

www.orionbooks.co.uk

To Jo Colwill at Cowslip Workshops –
for inspiration and Easter bunnies
G.A.

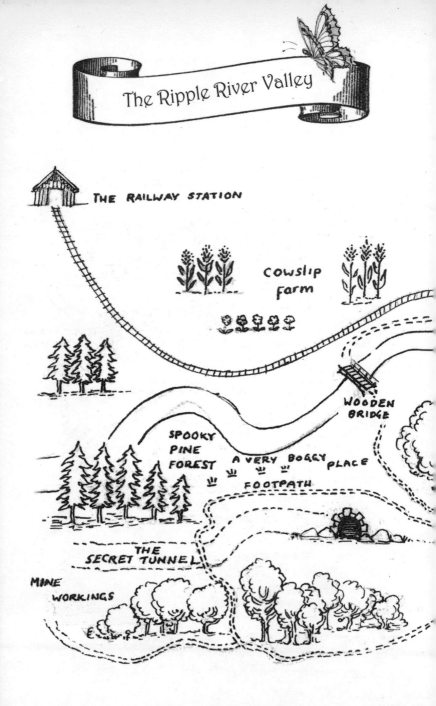

The Ripple River Valley

THE RAILWAY STATION

COWSLIP FARM

WOODEN BRIDGE

SPOOKY PINE FOREST

A VERY BOGGY PLACE

FOOTPATH

THE SECRET TUNNEL

MINE WORKINGS

THE CASTLE

OAKWOOD CROSSING

OLD STONE BRIDGE

FALLEN TREE

THE WARREN

ANOTHER BOGGY PLACE

FOOTPATH

FAIRWEATHER'S FARM PARK

Hunt the Acorns!

1

One fine spring morning Mellow
Longears was up-burrow, enjoying the
warmth of the sun on her grey-brown
fur. While she nibbled on a fresh green
dandelion leaf, Mellow kept an eye on
everything around her.

"You can never be too careful," she
said to a passing snail.

Not far off Barley Longears was sitting on his favourite tree stump. Mellow knew he would be looking out for danger, especially from their old enemy, Burdock the buzzard. The other day she'd spotted Burdock herself. The bird was perched high on a telegraph pole, waiting to catch a beetle, a mouse, or a rabbit. Mellow had frozen, not daring to breathe, until he'd flown away to hunt elsewhere.

Bramble, Bracken, Berry, Fern and Wisher were near the warren, playing a game of Tag-and-Tumble. Bramble, the biggest and boldest of the five young rabbits, was chasing his brothers and sisters in the meadow, his glossy black coat shining in the sun. Bramble was fearless! Mellow worried his adventurous nature might get him into trouble one day.

After a while, they all sat down to rest. Bramble couldn't keep still for long. He was soon on his paws again.

"Who's for a game of Hop-Back?" he said.

"We played that yesterday," said Bracken.

"And the day before," said Berry.

Wisher, the smallest of the Longears, was watching a puffy white cloud drift across the sky. Her silvery fur looked as soft as the little cloud. She was lost in a world of her own and didn't seem to hear what the others were saying.

"We could make daisy-chains," said Fern brightly.

Bramble rolled his eyes.

"You and your silly old daisies," he said.

Mellow sighed. She could tell Bramble was bored and restless.

"There must be *something* you can do together," she said.

Just then, Sylvia Squirrel came along. She looked upset.

"Hello," said Mellow. "What's the matter?"

"Oh," said Sylvia. "I buried some acorns and I can't remember where I put them. I'm sure they're around here somewhere . . ."

Bramble pricked his ears.

"I'll help you find them," he said.

"Will you?" said Sylvia. "That's very kind. Thank you."

"Hunt the Acorns!" announced Bramble. "It's my new game. Who wants to play?"

"I will," said Bracken, jumping up.

"Sounds good," said Berry.

"Wait for me," said Fern. "Coming, Wisher?"

Wisher blinked. "Where?" she said.

"To play Bramble's new game," said Fern. "Looking for Sylvia's acorns. It'll be fun."

Mellow smiled. She was pleased they wanted to help.

"Stay where I can see you," she said. "No running off."

"Quite right," said Sylvia. "There's a fox down by the river. I was climbing the big oak early this morning and saw him with my own eyes. He had a bushy red tail. Pointed nose. Sharp teeth . . ."

"Yes, I know what a fox looks like," said Mellow quickly.

"I don't," said Fern nervously.

"Don't worry, Marr," said Bramble. "If there's trouble, I'll send the signal Parr taught us."

He thumped his hind foot on the ground three times. *Thump, thump, thump!* "Anyway if I *do* meet that old fox, I'll pull his tail!"

"Ooo! You wouldn't dare," said Wisher.

Mellow half-believed he might. She looked hard at him when she said:

"Remember, sensible rabbits have careful habits!"

Bramble rushed about searching
for Sylvia's missing acorns.

"I hope I find them first," he said,
peering under a hawthorn bush.
"Ouch! The thorns are prickly."

He didn't find any acorns there, so he
looked for other places Sylvia might have
hidden them.

He dug holes in
a grassy bank,
turned over a
heap of leaves,
and scraped
soil from some
twisted tree
roots in the
hedgerow. But
he didn't find a

thing. Bramble's paws were sore and dirty
from digging. Then he heard a shout. It
was Fern, near the big oak.

"FOUND THEM!" she cried.

Bramble couldn't believe his ears. He
hurried over. Bracken, Berry and Wisher
were gathered round Fern, who was
proudly standing beside a pile of acorns.

"It isn't fair!" said Bramble, frowning at Fern. "Hunt the Acorns was my idea."

"Yes, it was a great idea," said Bracken.

"If you hadn't thought of it," said Berry, "the acorns might still be missing."

Wisher shook her head. "Why are you cross with Fern?" she asked Bramble.

He didn't have time to answer because Sylvia came running towards them with Mellow, closely followed by Barley. He looked worried.

"What's going on?" he said. "Has someone been hurt? Is something wrong?"

"All is well, Barley," said Sylvia. "Clever Fern has found my acorns!"

"I just dug around the oak and there they were," said Fern.

"Thank you, Fern," said Sylvia. She beamed at the other young rabbits. "It was very nice of you to help too." She scooped up the shiny acorns and scampered away.

Afterwards, Bramble just wanted to be by himself. He couldn't help feeling annoyed with Fern. He'd tried so hard to find the acorns, and it seemed his sister had found them so easily. He looked around to see what everyone else was doing.

Parr was back at his tree stump,
talking to his friend, Blinker Badger.

Marr was near
the warren, picking
flowers for her hat.

Fern,
Wisher, Berry
and Bracken were
busy eating.

When he thought no one would notice, Bramble slipped away. Only Bracken saw him go, and caught up with him down by the River Ripple.

"Don't be upset about the acorns," said Bracken. "Fern was lucky to find them, that's all."

"Why is Fern lucky at finding things and not me?" said Bramble. "Fern found a silver hare too. Remember?"

A while ago, when they'd stayed with their elders at Deep Burrow, Fern had discovered a missing silver hare, and everybody had been very pleased.

"Wisher helped her," said Bracken. "She heard voices and told Fern where to look."

Bramble knew it was true, but somehow it didn't make him feel any better. He was in a bad mood.

"*I* want to find something special," he said.

They stopped by a fallen tree across the river where the water swirled and bubbled over mossy rocks. A small animal came swimming towards them. She climbed out, shook her wet fur and smiled. It was Violet Vole.

"Hello," said Violet. "I couldn't help overhearing. I have some news that might interest you."

"Really?" said Bramble.

"It's a strange story," said Violet. "Something is happening at Fairweather's Farm Park today. Daisy Duck told me. She heard it from Gilbert Goose, and Mrs Woolly told him. A mystery, if you ask me.

No one is sure who they belong to
or where they came from . . ."

Bramble was confused.

"Please, Violet," he said. "What
are *they*?"

"Didn't I say?" said Violet. "Eggs.
Golden eggs. Enormous ones."

Bramble's eyes opened wide.

"Wriggly worms!" he cried. "Thank
you, Violet. They sound *really* special.
Come on, Bracken. We're going to look
for a golden egg!"

As Barley was talking to Blinker,
suddenly Burdock the buzzard appeared.
There was no mistaking the shape of his
outstretched wings circling overhead.

Barley gave the warning signal – *thump,*
thump, thump!

Nearby, three young Longears felt
the ground vibrate beneath their paws.
Mellow felt it too and dashed for home.

Barley and Mellow waited
by the warren. They saw
Burdock swoop low
and fast across
the meadow.
They saw the
flash of a white
bobbing tail.
Mellow held her breath. Barley trembled
with fear. Burdock missed his mark
and flew up. Then the blurred shapes
of rabbits came racing towards them,
darting right, left and right again. It was
Berry, Fern and Wisher and they dived
for the burrow.

"Where's Bramble?" said Barley.

"Where's Bracken?" said Mellow.

They were nowhere to be seen.

Golden Eggs
2

Mrs Woolly, who liked to know everyone's business, was puzzled. She'd just seen Fred Fairweather carrying a basket of eggs. This was odd because Mrs Woolly knew it was usually Jenny Fairweather who collected Hilda Hen's eggs each morning. Hilda had a habit of laying her white, brown and speckled eggs all over the farmyard. Mrs Woolly had once told her: "You're an untidy bird, Hilda."

To which Hilda had squawked: "I'm proud to be a Free Range hen. I'll lay my eggs where I choose!"

Mrs Woolly wasn't going to let Fred out of her sight. She ran to the gate and peered through the bars.

"How funny!" she said. "He's taking the eggs *out* of the basket and hiding them in the Play Park. Those can't be

Hilda's eggs. They're as gold as the sun."

She watched Fred hide the golden eggs under the trampoline, on top of the slide, around the sandpit, by the swings and on the climbing frame, until a young sheepdog came along wagging her tail. Mrs Woolly eyed the dog suspiciously.

"Who are you?" she said. "What are you doing?"

"I'm Sasha," said Sasha. "I'm looking for my master. Have you seen him?"

"I might have," said Mrs Woolly unhelpfully. She'd known a few sheepdogs in her time and hadn't trusted any of them. But Sasha seemed friendly enough, so she nodded towards the Play Park. "Fred Fairweather's over there, if that's who you mean. He's busy doing something with eggs."

Sasha was disappointed. She wanted to be doing her job, rounding up sheep. Then she had a bright idea.

"Could I round you up?" she asked.

"Bah!" said Mrs Woolly. "You'll do no such thing!" She glared at Sasha. "Clear off!"

Sasha ran back to the farmhouse, her tail between her legs. Maybe that wasn't such a good idea, she thought.

Some time later, Gilbert Goose came to see Mrs Woolly.

"Good goggly-oggly day," gabbled Gilbert. "Got any gossip?"

"Indeed I have," said Mrs Woolly. She told him about Fred and the golden eggs. "Do you know what's going on?"

"Afraid not-not-not," said Gilbert. "Here comes Hilda. Maybe she knows?"

But Hilda was no help either.

"Golden eggs?" she clucked. "Nothing to do with me. My eggs have all hatched. Look, I have eight beautiful chicks."

The fluffy chicks wobbled and wandered about in all directions.

"Goodness," said Mrs Woolly. "How do you keep them together?"

"I count them every now and then," said Hilda. "Now, as you can see I'm a busy bird. Lots to do. Goodbye." And off she went to the henhouse, her chicks trailing behind.

"Well," said Mrs Woolly. "Who laid those big golden eggs? A large bird, if I'm not mistaken. But why is Fred hiding them? It's all very mysterious."

Gilbert agreed. It was a good story and he waddled off to tell someone. It wasn't long before the golden eggs were the talk of the riverbank.

Sasha trotted into the farmhouse and went straight to her basket in the kitchen. She sighed a heavy sigh.

"I'm bored," she said.

Her mistress, Jenny Fairweather, was sitting at a large wooden table near an open window. She saw Sasha and said:

"Fred won't be long. He's meeting a group of school children off the train in a minute. I must finish sewing this Rag Bunny. It's a present. Just this piece for her face, then she's finished."

As Jenny reached for the little scrap of cloth a gust of wind blew through the window. Before she could catch it, the rag flew outside, tossed like a feather in the wind.

"Oh!" cried Jenny.

Sasha leapt to her paws.

"Woof, woof!" she barked. "Leave this to me. I'll track it down!"

Sasha ran outside, sniffing excitedly.

She was on the trail!

Skittles
Takes
a Ride
3

The Ripple Valley Steam Railway Station
was extra busy this morning. Florence
and Skittles, the two cats who lived at
The Station, walked up and down the
platform greeting the passengers – some
school children and their teachers. It was
very noisy. The big red steam engine,
SPITFIRE Number 47512, was hissing clouds
of steam. The children were laughing and
talking as they climbed aboard.

"What's going on?" said Florence loudly into Skittles' ear.

"I don't know," shouted Skittles. "I can't hear a thing!"

The cats stopped by a smart green and yellow carriage, full of excited girls and boys. Skittles sniffed.

"Fresh paint," he told Florence. "This one is new."

"Really?" said Florence, sitting to wash. She liked to keep her smooth black coat very clean. "All railway carriages look the same to me."

Curious, Skittles put a paw on the step.

"I'm going to look inside," he said. "I want to find out what's happening!"

"Don't be silly," said Florence. "The train is about to leave."

"I won't be long," said Skittles.

And he jumped on to the train.

He slipped under the wooden seats, then slowly made his way inside the carriage. The children were busy chattering. They didn't see the tabby with a smudgy black nose. But when he reached the end and could go no further, one little girl spotted him.

"Look!" she cried. "There's a cat. He's coming with us on the train!"

"Oh no I'm not," said Skittles.

He tried to make his escape, but the children were already reaching out to stroke his fur.

Then he heard SPITFIRE's shrill whistle.

Whooo-Wheeep!

The train gave a jolt, and they were off, rattling and clattering down the line.

By the time Skittles reached the open doorway, it was too late.

"Uh oh!" he said. He could see Florence getting smaller and smaller in the distance as the train gathered speed. *Clickerty-clack, clickerty-click,* went the wheels along the track. They were heading for Fairweather's Farm Park at the end of the line.

Florence sat on the empty platform and
watched the train disappear round
a bend in the track. She heard the whistle
blow again, then all was quiet. The
only sound was the slow *tick-tock* of the
station clock.

"Will I ever see Skittles again?"
she said.

Bramble led Bracken through a wood, along a well-worn path between tall trees and tangled bushes. Sometimes the two rabbits had to go round the trunk of a beech, scramble under a prickly stem, or hop over a log. Everywhere smelled of fresh new growth, and bluebells covered the woodland floor.

Bramble knew there were hidden dangers too. If they met trouble, there would be places to hide, but their adventure was risky all the same. Bracken was twice as worried. He stayed a few hops behind, stopping every now and then to warn Bramble.

"I-I th-th-think we should go back,"
he said. "I saw eyes in that hollybush!
Sylvia said she saw a fox this morning,
remember? Let's go home, Bramble,
please!"

Bramble did remember Sylvia's
warning, but he would never admit to
Bracken that he felt a bit nervous himself.
His only thought now was finding a
golden egg, and Bracken was holding
him up.

"Go back if you're scared," he said.
"I'm going on . . . wait, we're nearly there.
Aren't those the farm gates?"

Bracken looked to where Bramble was pointing. He remembered the time they'd both come to Fairweather's to rescue Berry. It had been winter and everything was covered with snow. It looked very different now.

"I think so," he said. "But what are those strange things on the grass? I don't remember seeing *them* before."

"Neither do I," said Bramble. "Maybe this is where we'll find a golden egg. Coming?"

Bracken nodded. He was afraid to go back on his own, and he didn't want Bramble to think he was a coward.

"Good," said Bramble, and meant it. He was glad Bracken had decided to stay. He took a quick look around for the fox. There was no sign or smell of him. Phew! he thought. He patted Bracken with his paw. "Don't worry. I'll look after you. Let's explore!"

They reached a wire fence and squeezed underneath. Bramble was trying to decide where they should start looking when a piercing shriek made them both jump.

Whooo-Wheeep!

They heard the deep rumbling of
something very big and very heavy
thundering along the valley.

It was the Red Dragon!

Too late, Bramble noticed they were
sitting very close to the monster's tracks.
The two felt the ground quake as the
Red Dragon charged down the line,
belching smoke and spitting sparks.
Hearts thumping, they looked around for
somewhere to hide.

The nearest thing Bramble saw was low and round – only a short dash away. "Run!" he shouted. "Follow me."

Skittles soon discovered he quite liked riding on the steam train. After the first few scary minutes when SPITFIRE had moved off, he'd settled down to enjoy the journey. The children seemed very happy to see him, although he thought one of the grown-ups looked worried. Oh dear! thought Skittles. I suppose Florence will be worrying about me too. It made him feel sad. He loved Florence more than anything. For a while, Skittles looked out of the window. As the train gathered speed, he saw trees and hedges and fields flying by, faster than he could ever have imagined. Then he curled up on a spare seat and spent the rest of the journey listening to the children's chatter. By the time SPITFIRE arrived huffing and puffing at Fairweather's Halt, Skittles knew all he needed to know about a special school visit to the farm. The children were going to hunt for Easter Eggs!

The Lost Chick

4

For a while, Bramble and Bracken felt safe inside their hiding place. There was just enough room for them to sit without their ears touching the roof. One side was open, so they could see what was going on. They took a few careful hops outside.

"The Red Dragon's stopped," said Bracken. "People-folk are climbing off his back."

"Yes," said Bramble, his eyes wide. "And they're coming this way!"

Bramble stared as children came running towards them. He scampered back to their hiding place. The children were peering into this and looking under that and shouting when they'd found something.

"I wonder if they're looking for golden eggs?" said Bramble.

"Maybe," said Bracken. "But if we stay here, it won't be long before they find us!"

Then Bramble heard a strange sound behind them.

Cheep-cheep! Cheep-cheep!

"Listen," he said.

Bramble and Bracken looked around. Their eyes were used to seeing in the darkness of their warren, but they couldn't see what was making the noise.

"I think it's a bird . . ." began Bramble, then stopped. *Something* had caught his eye. It was lying in the long grass, just outside their hiding place. His heart began to flutter. The object was shiny, egg-shaped and – golden.

"A GOLDEN EGG!" he cried.

"Brilliant!" said Bracken.

"I think I can reach it," said Bramble, stretching out his paw. He tapped, nudged, and patted the egg . . . but it wouldn't move. Then he gave it a push.

Bramble's golden egg toppled over, rolled gently down a slope and lay shining in the sunlight.

"Oh no!" said Bracken.

"I'm going after it," said Bramble.

"Wait!" said Bracken.

He had spotted a little girl. She ran over and picked up her prize.

"Look," she shouted happily to her friends. "I've found an Easter Egg!"

Bramble couldn't believe it. He'd

found and lost the special egg in less time than it took him to twitch a whisker.

"It's not fair . . ." he began. Then he stopped.

There was that noise again. Closer.
Louder.

Cheep-cheep! Cheep-cheep!

Bramble and Bracken spun round. A
tiny bird with fluffy yellow feathers and
an orange beak was
looking up at them.

"I'm lost," said
the bird.

Bramble
thought the little
bird looked as sad
as he'd felt just

now when he'd lost the golden egg. But
somehow the egg didn't seem important
any more.

"Don't worry," he said. "We'll help you."

Skittles settled down to wait at Fairweather's Halt – the stopping place for the Farm Park. He'd overheard the railway people talking about it once. It was at the end of the line and as far as SPITFIRE could go. He knew enough about the workings of the Railway Timetable to know the train would be returning to The Station. He just didn't know when.

To pass the time Skittles inspected the platform. There wasn't much to see – two lamp-posts, one wooden bench and a shelter where passengers could wait for the train. He decided it wasn't as interesting as The Station with its busy Booking Office, Gift Shop and Café. Skittles tried to remember all the things he'd learned from

the boys and girls on the way here so he
could tell Florence when he got home.

"They're going to hunt for Easter Eggs,"
he said. "Eggs made of chocolate. I think
that's right. Not real eggs. They'll visit the
newborn lambs and the baby chicks too.
Then they're having a picnic lunch . . ."

Lunch. That reminded Skittles he
was starting to feel hungry. His tummy
rumbled.

He thought of the dish of tasty fish he hoped would be waiting for him at The Station.

"I hope Florence won't eat my share!" he said.

Skittles was still thinking about food when a large brown hen appeared. She stopped and looked Skittles up and down, from the top of his ears to the tip of his tail.

"I'm Hilda," she said. "I know all the farm cats. You're a stranger."

Skittles nodded.

"I'm Skittles," he said. "I live at The Station at the other end of the line. I came on the train by mistake." He thought Hilda looked unfriendly and wondered why.

She fixed him with a beady eye.

"Do you know anything about a missing chick?"

"No," said Skittles. "Have you lost one?"

"Yes," said Hilda. "I had eight this morning. Now there are only seven. I think the bird who laid all these golden eggs has stolen my chick."

"Golden eggs?" said Skittles. Hm? They must be the ones the children were talking about. "Ha! You didn't think those eggs were real, did you? They're made of chocolate. People-folk call them Easter Eggs."

"Chocolate eggs?" cried Hilda. "What nonsense!"

With that Hilda went off to continue her search.

Bramble and Bracken did their best to comfort the little bird.

"What's your name?" asked Bramble.

"Custard," said Custard.

"Well, I'm Bramble," said Bramble. "This is my brother, Bracken."

"We're rabbits," said Bracken. "Um . . . please, what are you?"

"I'm a chick," said Custard. "And I want to go home." A tear trickled down his feathers.

"Where do you live?" asked Bracken.

"I don't know," said Custard.

"Do you live down a burrow like us?" said Bramble.

"What's a burrow?" said Custard.

Bramble wondered how they could help. He was sure Custard had a marr, but he didn't know what she looked like. Then he had an idea.

"Do you have any brothers and sisters?" he asked.

"Lots," said Custard, looking more cheerful.

"Do they look like you?" said Bramble.

"Yes," said Custard.

"Great," said Bramble. "All we have to do is find them. *They'll* take us to your marr!"

"You are clever!" said Bracken.

"Thank you," said Bramble.

He looked around. There were people-folk everywhere, but no yellow chicks. Then, across the clearing, he spotted some buildings.

"Let's start over there," he said. "I'll lead the way. Custard in the middle. Bracken behind."

They made slow progress because the chick couldn't walk very fast. The rabbits took a few hops at a time, stopping every now and then.

They counted every hop.

It took twenty hops to here.

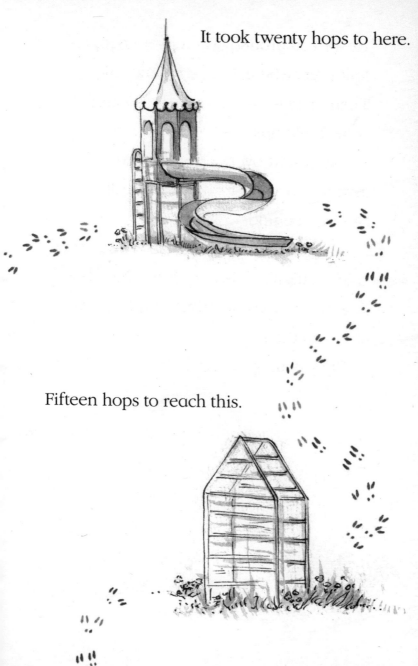

Fifteen hops to reach this.

Twelve more hops to these.

Then a quick dash across the sand.

Bramble was shaking sand from his paws when suddenly he heard

Thud-thud-thud!

He froze. Bracken and the chick froze too. People-folk were running towards them, their feet pounding the ground

Thud-thud-thud!

Bramble was sure they'd be seen, but the children charged by, heading for a wooden hut on the far side of the farmyard.

"Phew!" said Bramble.

"Phew!" said Bracken.

"Cheep!" said Custard.

It took only a few more hops to reach the farmyard. Bramble remembered when they'd come to find Berry here, and the night sky had been lit up with coloured lights. Now the barn, the pigsty and the stables were bathed in spring sunshine. And there, scratching about, were seven yellow chicks! They all looked like Custard. When the little lost chick saw them he chirped at the top of his voice. *"Cheep-cheep-cheep!"*

Hilda Hen rushed across the yard in a flurry of flying feathers.

"Oh, Custard. I've been looking for you *everywhere*," she said. "If it hadn't been for these kind rabbits, I might never have found you."

Bramble felt very pleased with himself.

At last he'd done something to be proud of. He thought Marr and Parr would be proud of him too.

"Thank you, thank you!" Hilda said to Bramble and Bracken.

"Glad we could help," said Bramble.

"Yes," said Bracken. "But we must hurry home now. Marr and Parr will be worried."

"Of course," said Hilda. "Can you find your way?"

Bramble told Hilda where they lived and she put them on the right path. Then, gathering together her eight beautiful chicks, Hilda marched them off to the henhouse.

The Raggy Bunny
5

Barley Longears paced up and down, tugging his ears.

"Where are they?" he said to Mellow for the ninety-ninth time.

"If I knew that," said Mellow, "I wouldn't be worrying my tail off!"

"If they're not back soon," said Barley. "I'll have to organise a search party."

Sylvia Squirrel was with them.

"Children are such a worry, aren't they?" she said.

"They've been gone quite a long time.
I saw a big fox down by the woods and I
shouldn't be surprised if . . ."

Barley wished Sylvia wouldn't keep
going on and on about that.

Nearby Berry, Fern and Wisher were
talking quietly together.

"If Bramble had found Sylvia's acorns, he might still be here," said Fern. "He was cross with me, remember?"

"It's not your fault," said Berry. "Is it, Wisher?"

"Um, yes," said Wisher. "I mean, no. Well, probably . . ."

Wisher had been half-listening, half-daydreaming. Her ears were tingling and she could hear a voice inside her head.

Wisher, Wisher, come and see –
The raggy bunny in a tree.

The words were puzzling:

Berry noticed Wisher had one of her faraway looks.

"What's up?" he said.

Wisher told them.

"What's a raggy bunny?" asked Fern.

"I don't know," said Wisher, "but I think it might help Bramble and Bracken."

A few minutes later, Violet Vole came rushing towards them. She looked flustered.

"I think I know where Bramble and Bracken are," she said. "I should have come sooner but I was busy with one thing and another and . . ."

"WHERE?" cried Barley. "Please, Violet. Tell us where they are!"

"Fairweather's Farm Park," said Violet. "I overheard Bramble down by the river. He wanted to find something special, you see? I'm afraid I told him about the golden eggs and he went off to look for them. Oh dear! I *have* been silly."

Barley couldn't make much sense of Violet's story. He was even more confused when Wisher told him about the raggy bunny.

"I don't really understand it myself," said Wisher.

"Well, one thing's clear," said Barley. "I'm going to Fairweather's. If Bramble and Bracken are in trouble, they'll need my help."

"May I go with you, Parr?" said Wisher. "My ears are tingling again."

Barley thought for a moment. Wisher had helped several times in the past by using her special powers.

"Yes," he said. "Maybe this er . . . raggy bunny thing will come in useful."

"Can we come, Parr?" said Berry and Fern.

"I think it would be better if you stayed here," said Barley. "You can keep watch for Bramble and Bracken in case they come back. Let's go, Wisher."

"Please be careful," said Mellow, waving them goodbye.

Barley and Wisher set off. They took a shortcut between the big oak and the holly bushes, and a few hops more brought them to a footpath.

The way ahead lay across open fields,
which Barley knew could be dangerous
for rabbits. He preferred to be within easy
reach of somewhere to hide.

"We must keep close to the hedge," he
said to Wisher.

As they went along, Wisher thought about her friend, Parsley Mole. Whenever she'd been lost, or wanted to go somewhere in a hurry, Parsley had taken her through one his tunnels. Parsley thought tunnels were the very best way to get about. And Wisher agreed with him. As they made their way by the hedgerow, Wisher half-hoped to see his whiskery snout pop out from a hole. I could get to Fairweather's in no time by tunnel, she thought. But she couldn't see any molehills and there was no sign of Parsley either.

Eventually, Barley and Wisher came to a bluebell wood. They took the path

between the trees, and soon they came to
the big gates of Fairweather's Farm Park.

"We're here," said Barley. "Can you
see Bramble and Bracken anywhere?"

There was no reply. Barley turned
round. Wisher was staring at
something in a tree.

"Look, Parr," she said.
"What's that?"

Something was flapping
in the breeze, as if it was
waving at her. Wisher
reached up, but it was
too high.

"Here," said
Barley. "Let me
help you."

Barley bent over and Wisher climbed on to his back. She stood up and unhooked the little rag. Wisher gave a gasp of surprise. Smiling out from the raggy cloth was the face of – a rabbit.

Wisher, Wisher, come and see –
The raggy bunny in a tree.

Sasha's on the Trail
6

Nose to the ground. *Sniff, sniff, sniff!*
Sasha the sheepdog was on the trail.
The raggy cloth had a scent of its own. It
smelled like ripened corn and new-mown
hay. *Sniff, sniff, sniff!* She was glad to be
doing something useful.

"If I can't round up sheep for my
master," she said, as she trotted up a
path near the railway line, "I'll help my
mistress instead."

Approaching a wood, Sasha's nose
was filled with the smell of trees, damp
earth, leaves . . . and something else. She
wagged her tail with excitement. *Sniff,
sniff!* Sasha could smell – RABBIT!

She followed the trail down a
woodland path until, sure enough,

hopping along in front of her, were two rabbits. The larger one was black, and the other was gingery-brown.

"WOOF! WOOF!" said Sasha, and she chased after them.

Bramble and Bracken hurried along a path by the Red Dragon's tracks. Hilda Hen had told them it was the quickest way back to the wood. But first they had to pass the place where the Red Dragon had stopped. They could hear him huffing and hissing, and making clouds of steam.

"Oooo!" said Bracken. "I wish we didn't have to go so near him."

"There's no other way," said Bramble. "But remember what Parr told us? The Red

Dragon never leaves his tracks. We'll be all right if we stay on this path."

They hopped quickly on, and were almost clear of the smoky beast when they caught sight of a small animal, sitting right beside the monster. The animal waved a friendly greeting, but the rabbits were too scared to stop.

"Who was that?" said Bracken, when they'd run a safe distance from the Red Dragon.

"I've no idea," said Bramble. "But he was very brave!"

Just then from behind, came a terrifying sound. *WOOF! WOOF!* Bramble knew without looking it was a dog.

It stopped them in their tracks. The dog was coming closer. They could hear it crashing through the undergrowth, yelping with excitement.

"Run," said Bramble. "Make for a hole. A bush. Anywhere. Now!"

Sasha spotted the flash of two fluffy tails as the rabbits leapt from the path. Up went her tail. Down went her nose.

"This is fun," she said, bounding after them.

Sasha soon discovered that chasing rabbits was very different to rounding up sheep. The woolly creatures usually stayed together, but the two rabbits darted this way and that, quick as anything. And now, to confuse matters, Sasha could smell even *more* rabbits. *Sniff, sniff!* There was something else too. Ripened corn and new-mown hay – the very thing she'd been tracking for her mistress, Jenny Fairweather.

What she saw next brought Sasha skidding to a stop.

Wisher and Barley stared in amazement. Everything happened so fast. Suddenly Bramble and Bracken were racing towards them. A long-haired dog was close behind and getting closer. And chasing after them all was an even more frightening sight. A large white goose was honking and flapping his wings and making a terrible noise.

HONK-HONK-HONK!

Wisher stood her ground.

Something told her she would be all right. The smiling rabbity face on the cloth was reassuring, and she held it tight.

Barley was very frightened. Here he was with Bramble, Bracken and Wisher, face to face with a dog and an angry-looking bird. His head whirled.

"Parr!" shouted Bramble.

"Wisher!" shouted Bracken.

"Woof!" said Sasha, one eye fixed firmly on the flapping rag. She had lost interest in Bramble and Bracken now. Then she saw Gilbert Goose. He looked very cross.

"Sasha!" screeched Gilbert. "What were you doing chasing these poor rabbity-abbity-rabbits? They found Hilda's lost chick and brought him home."

"Sorry," said Sasha, her tail drooping. "One rabbit looks much like another to me."

"The Longears family are our friends," said Gilbert. "From now on, stick to rounding up sheep, young uppity-puppity-pup!"

"Yes," said Sasha. "I promise. She turned to Wisher and asked *very* politely:

"May I have that cloth? It belongs to my mistress, Jenny."

"Of c-c-course," said Wisher. She'd never been this close to a dog before.

Plucking up her courage, Wisher held it out and Sasha took the rag gently from her paw.

"Thank you," she said.

Then Sasha and Gilbert hurried back to the farm. They both had a good tale to tell.

Bramble's
Special
Story
7

"I never have and never *will* trust a dog," said Barley, when he was sure Sasha had gone. "Now everybody, back to the warren!"

"I can't wait to get home," said Bracken.

"Me too," said Wisher. She was still trembling from her close encounter with a dog, even though Sasha hadn't meant her any harm.

"I've got a lot to tell you, Parr," said Bramble.

"Yes, you have!" said Barley. "Your marr and I have been worrying our whiskers off about you and Bracken. Violet Vole told us a very strange tale about some golden eggs. And what's all this about a lost chick?"

On the way home, Bramble entertained everyone with his adventures.

"It started with Sylvia Squirrel's acorns . . ." he began. When he got to the part where they'd met Parr and Wisher in the wood, he looked puzzled. "How did you know where we were?"

"We didn't . . ." began Barley and stopped.

He looked at Wisher. "Maybe we did?"

"My ears were tingling," Wisher told Bramble. "A voice gave me a weird message and we found you. I don't really understand how it happened."

"You and your funny ears!" said Bramble. He gave Wisher a big smile. "If Sasha hadn't spotted that rag, she'd still be chasing us!"

"That's true," said Barley. "You had a lucky escape."

Just then they heard a loud

Whooo-Wheeep!

A few seconds later, the Red Dragon came rushing down his tracks. He flew by so fast that the wind flattened their fur.

"He's in a hurry to get home," said Wisher.

"Look, Bracken," said Bramble, pointing to the back of the monster. "There's the animal we saw earlier. He's waving to us again."

And this time they all waved back.

Mellow was waiting anxiously at the warren. Fern and Berry kept a look-out, chasing each other around the big oak to pass the time.

When she couldn't wait any longer, Mellow hopped down to the river to see if anyone had seen Barley and the others. The first friend she met was Daisy Duck, who told her some alarming news.

"You'll never believe it," said Daisy. "Gilbert Goose told me and he heard it from Mrs Woolly, so it must be true. Such goings on at Fairweather's today. Poor Bramble and Bracken were nearly

run over by a giant Easter Egg. It rolled
down a hill and nearly squashed them.
Bramble found some golden chicks. Ten
or twelve at least. And they both had a
narrow escape from a sheep. Or was it a
dog? It may have been both? Yes! They
had to run for their lives from a flock of
angry sheep *and* a pack of dogs!"

Mellow's eyes grew wider and wider as Daisy told her story, but she did wonder if any of it could possibly be true. Then she spotted a little band of rabbits, hopping along the riverbank. When they saw Mellow, they ran as fast as they could to meet her.

"I've been hearing some extraordinary tales," she said. "I can't wait to hear what really happened!"

That night, when Mellow came to say goodnight, Bramble said, "I'm glad I found a golden egg, Marr. But finding the little lost chick was even better!"

"I'm very proud of you," said Mellow. "And so is Parr."

And she kissed him on the nose.